Knick Knack

Clella Bay Murray

AuthorHouse™
1663 Liberty Drive
Bloomington, IN 47403
www.authorhouse.com
Phone: 1 (800) 839-8640

Published by AuthorHouse 08/22/2018

ISBN: 978-1-5462-5521-5 (sc)
ISBN: 978-1-5462-5523-9 (hc)
ISBN: 978-1-5462-5522-2 (e)

Library of Congress Control Number: 2018909721

Print information available on the last page.

authorHOUSE®

Dedicated to
Richard, Ada, Annette

Acknowledgements

My especial gratitude goes to Richard Murray, as always my best friend and main supporter. Thanks to Alice Condon for encouragement to write the story of Knick Knack. Special thanks to Barbara Valbuena for careful editing of the book. Grateful thanks to Anna Bellenger for the imaginative illustrations. Always appreciation to Ada Koch and Annette Orella for reviews and suggestions. Heartfelt thanks to Mary Abarquez, Jose Ortega, and all those at AuthorHouse who brought the book to completion.

Knick Knack

Once upon a time in Santa Claus Land, North Pole, there lived an elf named Knick Knack. He got his name from the sound his bright red hammer made whenever he pounded a piece of wood. If you listened long enough the mallet noise became a tune: knick, knack, knick, knack. Sometimes the other elves would sing along to the beat. Knick Knack was as fat and red of nose as Santa himself, but alas, he was only one foot tall. Knick Knack was happy, generous and kind just as all the people at Santa Claus Land are obliged to be, but as so many of us, he had a fault. He loved to play practical jokes. Now everyone knows elves are supposed to be serious and hardworking. Knick Knack was indeed good at his job and he worked hard. He tried and tried to be serious and settle down, but unfortunately, when an opportunity presented itself, poor little Knick Knack took off.

Monday he mixed up the colors in the dolls paint jars. All the golden haired babies had red eyes and green noses and the toy soldiers wound up with purple moustaches.

Tuesday night when all the elves were sleeping Knick Knack sewed up their sleeves. Elves sleep VERY soundly! The next morning not a single elf could get undressed or dressed. They couldn't even turn the knob to open the door to call Santa or worse yet, they couldn't eat breakfast!

But the last straw was the day Knick Knack put pepper in the reindeer's food. Every time they sneezed, Santa would fall out of the sleigh. Luckily, Santa is very amplify padded and he always landed on a cloud.

"Something must be done, Santa," steamed Fuss the chief elf. "He's ruining morale. All the elves laugh instead of toil. Today he put tacks on my high stool! It took three elves all morning to get the tacks out of my – um- um- me. I've had to do all my jobs standing up – and at my age I like to do my chores sitting down!!"

Santa couldn't help but smile at the thought of Fuss jumping from a stool covered with tacks, but he hid it kindly with a cough. "What do you suggest, Fuss?"

"We must teach Knick Knack a lesson — for his own good, of course," Fuss drew himself up importantly. "Perhaps if you would take him to earth before Christmas, after Thanksgiving maybe, and see if he could accomplish something — do a good, honest day's labor without any foolishness. Then he could come back." Having given this advice, Fuss plopped into a chair only to jump up again. His seat was still a little tender.

Santa nodded thoughtfully, "We'll see, Fuss. We'll see." After much thought, and walking back and forth, Santa agreed with Fuss. That is how Knick Knack came to be set down on the edge of Covered Bridge Farms the day after Thanksgiving. Santa gave Knick Knack a sack lunch, a set of tools, a big hug and took off quickly, for no one should see Santa before Christmas, especially when he is blowing his nose and wiping a tear from his eye.

Knick Knack looked about himself with interest. The trees were still green, quite different from the snow-clad fields of Santa Claus Land. Poor, dejected Knick Knack sat down on a tree stump to have some lunch. He was ready to take a bite of last year's Christmas fruit cake, the elves didn't like it and a lot was always left over, when he heard voices. He scooted behind a large gooseberry bush just as two children came down the road.

"Do you really think we won't get anything for Christmas again this year? I've certainly been good." Karl asked his sister.

Karen smiled at him, "You'll get one present – from me – I'm making it myself."

"Isn't that just like a dumb girl," thought Karl. "I want toys and stuff and she's probably knitting me something that won't fit and be some sissy color!" But his little sister looked so happy he didn't say anything, he just frowned at his shoes.

"This year Papa has a job, and we have food enough for all winter and fire wood and Mama is better. So we don't need any more," Karen started to hum.

In spite of himself, Karl felt better. "You're a good person, Karen. I know you want a doll or dishes as much as I want a soldier or a sled. I promise I won't complain again." Arm-in-arm they walked back up the road.

Knick Knack stepped from his hiding place and scratched his head. Before this he had only made toys, he had never seen the children get them. "I thought all good kids got what they wanted at Christmas. I thought only bad kids didn't get presents. Karen seems like a nice little girl. By golly! She'll have her doll, and dishes, and a soldier and sled for the little man, or my name is not Knick Knack!" He went on muttering to himself as he trotted off into a nearby woods and with great gusto started to saw down the first tree he came to. Luckily, it was a soft white pine.

Knick Knack was one of those people who would joke and play pranks all the time unless someone or something touches their heart and they have something to work for and work he did! Knick Knack laid his tools out on the ground and got busy. First he shaped legs, arms and a body for a round little lady doll out of a chuck of wood from the soft pine tree. Then a crude set of dishes appeared. He whistled as he whittled and sanded. Soon the dolls skin was silky smooth and the dishes took on graceful little shapes. Next he started on a soldier, stiff and tall and a magnificent sled six inches longer than usual! For paint he used stain from the walnuts, grass, berries and saffron.

All the creatures of the forest came to see what he was doing. "What a nice thing to do. All my wise thoughts, and after a cup of coffee, I think we should help." Oscar Owl hooted. So it happened a blue bird landed on Knick Knack's shoulder. "I'm Betty. I'll make the doll a hat out of my feathers," she chirped "and I'll get some yellow feathers from Celia Chickadee for her hair."

 "Oh, My! Thank you," said Knick Knack. He was surprised. A big black spider crawled up Knick Knack's leg. "I'm Sam. We've heard what you're doing and the missus and her lady friends want to spin a lovely, lacy dress. I'll put some sap glue on it so it won't fall apart."

Two squirrels dug up some old discarded drainage pipes they had found nearby and dragged them over. "We're Tit and Tack and thought these would make nice runners for the sled once they're split, sanded, and smoothed over. We'll do it. It's how we keep our teeth sharp and clean." They smiled a big smile showing their pearly, white teeth. Knick Knack was overcome by all their kindness. With tears in his eyes he said, "Thank you. Thank you."

Everyone went to work. The forest had never heard such chatter, squeaks and laughter. Knick Knack thanked heaven when everyone ate the stale fruit cake. They must have been very hungry because it went fast! Two days before Christmas the toys were finished and Knick Knack, the animals and birds eyed their accomplishment with pride. Santa's most masterly elves could not have done better. On Christmas eve Knick Knack stole quietly to the little home in the woods. After everyone was asleep, he placed the gifts beside the fireplace. He took up watch by one of the windows. Knick Knack was so absorbed he didn't notice anyone walking up behind him. When a big furry mitten tapped him on the shoulder he jumped as high as the roof! "WHAT?" he shouted.

"Shhhh." laughed a familiar voice. Santa was returning from his midnight ride. "Keep your voice down, you'll wake them!" he said. Santa peeked in at the toys by the fireplace. "Well done, Knick Knack. You've certainly proved yourself. Above and beyond! Even Fuss will welcome you back at your place in the elf shop. I'm proud of you! Now, hop on the sleigh and I'll take you home. Fast now before the first ray of light."

Knick Knack looked at Santa and then back at the toys by the fireplace. He knew deep in his heart what he must do. "No, Santa." he said with tears in his eyes, "I'll miss you and Fuss, maybe not Fuss so much, but all the other elves. I do hope to see you each Christmas Eve, please? You see, there are good children here on earth who need me for toys, not just for Christmas but birthdays and all big important days, too. Some don't have anyone to write you letters for them and they are forgotten."

Santa looked at the little elf with a deepened respect, "You have received the greatest gift of all in return for your work, Knick Knack. You have found you are needed." A cock's crow sounded loud and clear. Santa hugged the little fellow and jumped to his sleigh. "Oops, off we go! See you next Christmas eve. That's a promise!"

"Wait," shouted Knick Knack, "I have a gift for Fuss." He held up a wooden puzzle. "This is special. No matter how often or how many ways he puts it together, there will always be one piece missing," he laughed.

Santa looked at the puzzle in his hand and gave a big guffaw, his stomach shook and tears ran down his check at the thought of Fuss's frustration, but time was wasting. Santa jumped on his sleigh, shouted, "Merry Christmas." And all the way to the North Pole people heard him laugh, "Ho, Ho, Ho.".

Knick Knack turned and peeked again through the window. He saw the children come into the room, stop and stare and then began to jump for joy and holler out their surprise and hug each other.. He watched for a while and then blew his nose, wiped his eyes, turned, and walked down the path.

All the forest animals and birds cried, "Wait! We want to come, too, and make toys."

Knick Knack smiled, "Okay, but no practical jokes, well, hmmm, maybe just a few once and a while when I go back to the North Pole." From that day on Knick Knack and his friends now roam the world watching for children who need them. If you listen very closely and watch carefully you may hear a tiny little knick knack or see the tiniest bit of a red nose in a woods or near a sheltered place. You will know Knick Knack and his friends are busy at work when you hear the knick knack, knick knack of his hammer. Best watch out for a practical joke Knick Knack may play on YOU some Christmas Eve!

The End

Printed in the United States
By Bookmasters